Silly Goose and Daft Duck Play Hide-and-Seek

Sally Grindley

Illustrated by Adrian Reynolds

Silly Goose and Daft Duck went for a walk in the woods. Suddenly, Silly Goose held on to Daft Duck's wing and said, "I think someone's following us."

They looked round,

but there was no-one there.

"Silly me," said Silly Goose,

"I must be imagining things."

They walked on again.

Suddenly, Daft Duck leapt in the air and said,

"I heard a twig snap."

They turned slowly round and
saw Clever Fox tiptoeing away.

Cooeee!

"We can see you!" called Silly Goose.

"Are you playing hide-and-seek?"

"Can we play too?" said Daft Duck.

"All right," said Clever Fox.

He smiled a hungry smile.

"You hide while I count to five."

One!

Silly Goose tried to **squeeze** inside a hollow log . . .

but she was too **fat**.

Two!

Daft Duck
tried to climb
a tree . . .
but
he was scared
of heights.

Three!

Silly Goose crawled under a holly bush . . . **but** it was much too **prickly**.

Four!

Daft Duck jumped in the river . . .

. . . but it was too cold.

Five!

Silly Goose scuttled under a pile of leaves.

Coming, ready or not!

Daft Duck squatted behind
a pile of stones.

"Which one shall I eat first?" sniggered Clever Fox.

"The silly goose or the daft duck?"

He began to look for them.

Daft Duck giggled.

Silly Goose sneezed.

Clever Fox crept up behind Daft Duck.

Grizzly Bear crept up behind Clever Fox.

BOoooooo! boomed Grizzly Bear.

Aaaaaaaah!

yelled Clever Fox and he shot
off out of the woods.

"Just as well I came along when I did,"
chuckled Grizzly Bear.

"You frightened our friend,"
grumbled Silly Goose.

"And spoilt our game," said Daft Duck.

"You'll have to play instead."

One

Two

Three

Four

Five

Coming, ready or not!

called Silly Goose and Daft Duck.